Published by Darf Children's Books
An imprint of Darf Publishers Ltd
277 West End Lane
West Hampstead
London
NW6 1QS

Wilbert
By Bárður Oskarsson

Originally published as *Wilbert*

Translated by Marita Thomsen
Edited by Beth Cox

Storyline and illustrations © 2016 Bárður Oskarsson

The moral right of the author has been asserted

All rights reserved

This book is sold subject to the condition that it shall not, by way of trade or otherwise, be lent, resold, hired out, or otherwise circulated without the publisher's prior consent in any form of binding or cover other than that in which it is published and without a similar condition, including this condition, being imposed on the subsequent purchaser.

A catalogue record of this book is available from the British Library.

Printed and bound in China by Imago

ISBN-13: 978-1-85077-325-2

www.darfpublishers.co.uk

BÁRÐUR OSKARSSON

WILBERT

darf
children's
books

1, 2, 3 ...

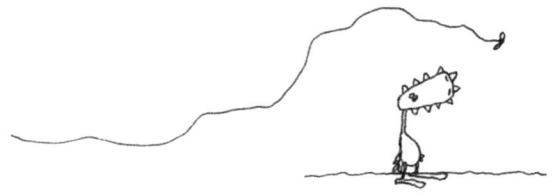

"Ready or not, here I come!"

...

...

"Hello!" said Rat. "I'm looking for my friend, Wilbert. Have you seen him?"

"Nope..." said Crocodile.

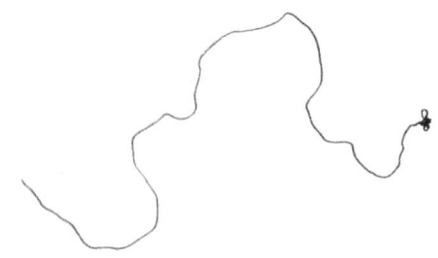

"If you tell me what he looks like, maybe I can help you find him," said Crocodile.

"Well, he looks a lot like me, but a bit taller."

"Oh him," said Crocodile. "Yes, I saw him."

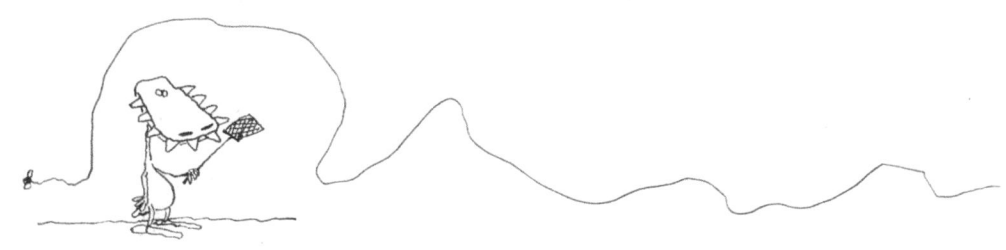

"I ate him!"

"NOOOOO!" yelled Rat.

She felt scared and sad and angry all at once.

"Ha ha!" laughed Crocodile. "Got you! I didn't really eat him."

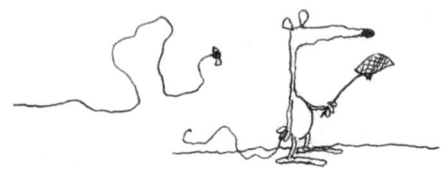

"Look," said Crocodile, opening her mouth as wide as she could. "I haven't eaten anyone."

"But I could help you look. Let's see if he's hiding over there."

They looked and looked, but they couldn't find Wilbert.

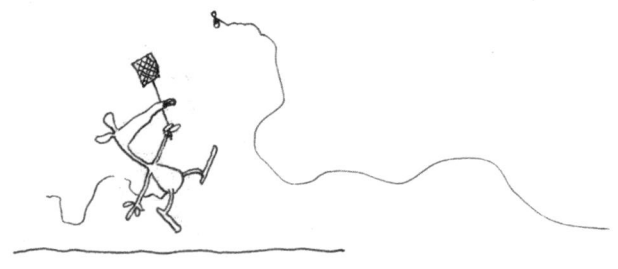

"There he is!" Rat whispered. "Over there, behind that big tree."

Crocodile looked long and hard at the tree, then she looked around the tree, but she couldn't see any sign of Wilbert.

"I can't see him," she said. "Where is he?"

"Hey, Wilbert!" Rat shouted. "I can see you! You're it!"

"Can you see Wilbert's ears?" Rat asked Crocodile.

"No," said Crocodile.

"Hey, Wilbert," shouted Rat. "Crocodile helped me and we found you."

Crocodile still couldn't see anyone.

"Is Wilbert still standing behind the tree?" she asked Rat.

"No," said Rat. "He's right in front of us now."

Wilbert and Rat chatted for a bit. Then they went back to playing hide and seek.

They let Crocodile play too.

But even though Crocodile found Rat every time, Rat always had to help Crocodile find Wilbert.